Pink Boat, Pink Car

Written and illustrated by
Laura Hambleton

Collins

Kit had a pink car.

Tom had a pink boat.

They took turns.

5

Ella took them.

They did not join in.

Ella did not feel good.

A story map

 After reading

Letters and Sounds: Phase 3

Word count: 52

Focus phonemes: /ar/ /ow/ /oa/ /oo/ /oo/ /ure/ /ur/ /oi/ /air/ /ee/

Common exception words: my, I, the, are, they, your, we

Curriculum links: Personal, Social and Emotional Development: Managing feelings and behaviour; Making relationships

Early learning goals: Listening and attention: listen attentively in a range of situations, listen to stories, accurately anticipating key events and respond to what they hear with relevant comments, questions or actions; Reading: read and understand simple sentences; use phonic knowledge to decode regular words and read them aloud accurately; read some common irregular words

Developing fluency

- Your child may enjoy hearing you read the story.
- Look at the story map on pages 14–15 and ask your child to retell the story in their own words.

Phonic practice

- Look at the word **boat** together. Segment it into its three phonemes b/oa/t. Point to /oa/ and practise the sound, then blend the phonemes together.
- Do the same with the following words:

  c/ar

  s/ure

  t/ur/n

  f/air

Extending vocabulary

- Ask your child:
  - Can you think of another word for 'taking turns' when you and a friend are playing with a toy? (*sharing*)
  - Can you think of another word for 'boat'? (*ship, yacht*)